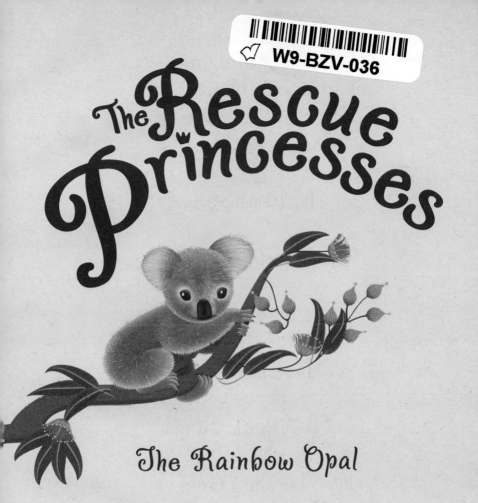

The Rescue Princesses

The Rainbow Opal

More amazing
animal adventures!

The Secret Promise

The Wishing Pearl

The Moonlight Mystery

The Stolen Crystals

The Snow Jewel

The Magic Rings

The Lost Gold

The Shimmering Stone

The Silver Locket

The Ice Diamond

The Rescue Princesses

The Rainbow Opal

❤ **PAULA HARRISON** ❤

Scholastic Inc.

For Esther Mary Scourse
and her koalas, Koko and Koco

ISBN 978-0-545-66166-9

12 11 10 9 8 7 6 5 4 3 2 1   14 15 16 17 18 19/0

Printed in the U.S.A.   40
First printing, June 2014

CHAPTER ONE

Exploring the Woods

Princess Summer raced downstairs, her golden hair bouncing on her shoulders. She was so excited that her friends had come to visit! Jumping down the last two steps, she ran toward the door.

Summer's mom, the queen of Mirrania, came into the hallway. "Wait a minute, Summer! Where are you going?"

"I'm taking my friends to the woods to show them all the animals," said Summer.

"What about your hair?" said the queen. "Have you brushed it?"

"I think I did." Summer flicked back her hair. "I'm sure it looks all right, anyway."

The queen sighed. "Well, don't forget that the photographer's coming today."

"I won't. See you later!" Summer rushed out the door.

The sun beat down on the walls and pointed towers of the palace. Straight ahead lay a neat lawn full of bright flowers, with the wild forest just beyond.

Three princesses were waiting for Summer at the bottom of the palace steps. Maya was smiling shyly, her dark braid hanging over her shoulder. Lottie was practicing cartwheels on the grass. Rosalind stood with her arms folded, tapping her foot impatiently.

Summer's heart lifted as she ran toward them. She'd met the girls at

Maya's palace, in the kingdom of Lepari. They had climbed a steep mountain to rescue a snow leopard cub from terrible danger. It had been an amazing adventure!

Lottie and Rosalind had explained that they'd set up a secret club for rescuing animals and it was called the Rescue Princesses. She'd felt so happy when they'd asked her to join. She loved animals and always wanted to help them. Now she had friends who felt that way, too!

Each Rescue Princess wore a ring with a magical jewel. The jewels let them call one another when they found an animal in trouble. Summer's jewel was a beautiful purple amethyst. She touched it and smiled.

Lottie stopped cartwheeling and looked at Summer. The breeze ruffled her curly red hair. "We're all ready, Summer! What did you want to show us?"

"Lots of things!" replied Summer. "There's a whole forest full of animals and birds beyond that gate." She pointed to an old wooden gate in the corner. "It was dark when you all arrived yesterday, so I couldn't show it to you. But I know you'll like it. We have amazing animals here in Mirrania. There are kangaroos, possums, and koalas, and in the evening, you can see bats flying around."

"Awesome!" cried Lottie.

"Oh, I almost forgot! First of all, you have to meet Kanga." Summer gazed around the garden, calling out, "Kanga? Where are you?"

A blue-and-yellow parrot flew down to the topmost step by the front door. He put his head to one side and looked at the girls.

"Oh yes! I remember you telling us you had a pet parrot," said Rosalind, smoothing her short blond hair. "But why do you call him Kanga? Isn't that a better name for a kangaroo?"

Kanga opened his beak and gave a loud squawk. Then he bounced down the palace steps one by one. He looked so funny that the girls had to laugh.

"You see! That's why I called him Kanga," said Summer. "Sometimes he bounces along instead of flying."

"He's a parrot that acts like a kangaroo!" Lottie grinned. "I think I'm going to like this place!"

Kanga hopped a few more times before spreading his wings and flying up to Summer's shoulder. "Are you ready for an adventure, Kanga?" she asked him.

Kanga bobbed his head in reply.

The princesses followed Summer

through the gate that led out into the woods. They stepped over tangled bushes and pushed their way through the trees. Their shoes scuffed up the reddish earth. High in the branches, birds were calling to one another. One flew past with a low, swooping cry.

"It sounds so strange out here," murmured Maya.

"It smells different, too," said Lottie. "It's a fresh sort of smell — I really like it!"

Rosalind jumped as a furry animal with a bushy tail ran past. "Summer! What's that?"

"It's a brush-tailed possum," Summer told her. "There's a whole family of them living in here."

The little possum poked its pink nose out of the middle of a bush, and its whiskers quivered. Rosalind bent down to look. "I like him. He's cute," she decided.

"I know an animal that's even cuter," said Summer. "Come and see!"

With Kanga still riding on her shoulder, she went over to a tall tree with a pale trunk and blue-gray leaves. "See that furry gray animal halfway up? That's a mother koala with her baby on her back. We call the baby a joey."

At the sound of Summer's voice, the baby koala turned its head and looked down at the girls with big black eyes.

"He's gorgeous!" cried Maya. "Look at his beautiful fur and fluffy ears!"

Rosalind folded her arms. "I still like the possum best."

"I've always wanted to see a koala," said Lottie. "I didn't know they carried their babies on their backs like that."

"They only do that once the joey's old enough to live outside his mother's pouch." Summer saw their puzzled faces and added, "The pouch is like a furry pocket on her stomach."

"Is the baby koala all right?" said Maya suddenly. "I thought I saw him drop one arm, as if he was going to let go."

Summer looked up, shading her eyes. "Don't worry. He's used to riding on his mother's back."

As they watched, the mother koala pulled a bunch of leaves off the tree and began eating them. Then a rumbling noise started up in the distance. It quickly grew into the deafening growl of a motorcycle. Kanga ruffled his feathers and looked alarmed as the sound came closer. Then suddenly it stopped.

Summer frowned. "That sounds like a motorcycle. I wonder who it is."

"I want to find more koalas." Lottie ran to the next tree. "They're my new favorite animal!"

"Why don't we go farther into the woods —" began Summer, but she broke off as she heard her mom's voice. "Oh no! My mom's calling me. I bet the sound of the motorcycle was the photographer arriving. Now I have to go and have my photo taken." She made a face.

"What's wrong?" asked Rosalind. "Don't you like having your picture taken?"

"I don't usually mind," replied Summer. "But this isn't a normal photo. It's something much worse! In our kingdom, every prince or princess has a special picture taken after their tenth birthday. Everyone in the kingdom sees it, and it even gets shown on TV!"

Just then, the queen of Mirrania appeared at the edge of the trees. Her face was pink, and her crown had slipped sideways on her neat hair. "Summer, why are you taking so long? Bill Fleck has arrived, and he's setting up his camera right now."

Kanga gave a loud squawk and flew away to the top of the highest tree.

Summer sighed. "I've got to go," she told the other princesses. "Stay here and watch the animals if you want. You can still have fun even if I can't!"

CHAPTER TWO

The Royal Photo

Summer reluctantly followed her mom into the palace drawing room. Dark red sofas stood at one side of the room, and velvet curtains hung at the windows.

The photographer, who had a bristly mustache and a fancy bow tie, had already set up the camera on its stand. He was busily polishing the camera lens with a small yellow cloth.

"My dear princess!" The photographer bowed low, and his yellow cloth swept the floor. "I'm Bill Fleck, and I'm absolutely delighted to meet you. It's like a dream come true!"

"Er . . . thanks." Summer curtsied back. She hoped he would take the photo really quickly. Then she could go back outside with her friends. "Where should I go? Over here by the sofa?"

"Just a moment, Summer." The queen hurried forward. "We need to organize this carefully. After all, this is a very important photo."

"Yes, that's right!" Bill nodded. "It's your tenth birthday portrait. So it'll be shown to the whole kingdom and hung in the Royal Gallery."

Summer sighed. "Yes, I know! But —"

"So you have to look absolutely perfect," her mom broke in. "I've prepared some things that will help." She bustled over to a wooden chest and pulled the lid open.

Summer's mouth dropped open as her mom took out a red robe with a furry white lining and a chunky gold crown. "Do you really want me to wear those?"

The queen smiled. "You'll look wonderful! But first of all you need to run upstairs and put this on." She took down a dress that had been hanging on the back of the door. It had orange and lime-green stripes all over it, even across the sleeves. Worst of all, it had lacy ruffles around the huge skirt.

Summer stared at it in horror. She couldn't imagine wearing anything worse. "But I won't be able to walk in that! And I won't look like *me* anymore!"

"Don't be silly!" said her mom, handing her the dress. "Of course you'll still look like you. Go and put it on, please."

Summer took the dress and trailed out of the room. She passed her dad in the hallway, and the king's eyebrows rose when he saw the frilly dress.

"Are you getting ready for the photo?" he asked.

Summer nodded. "Mom wants the picture taken right now."

"I see." The king frowned a little. "I think I'll go and see what your mom has in mind."

Summer dragged herself up the stairs to her bedroom. She changed into the awful dress and looked at herself in the mirror. The thought of the whole kingdom seeing her like this made her stomach turn over. The top of the dress was too tight, and the skirt tangled around her ankles. The ruffles were horribly itchy, scratching her legs in a really annoying way.

She had much nicer dresses, which were short and easy to run and climb in. Why couldn't she wear one of those?

To cheer herself up, she got out the small green jewelry box that had her favorite opal necklace inside. At least she would wear one thing that she really liked!

But before she could get the necklace out, there was a knock at the door. Summer swallowed. That would be her mom wanting her to hurry up.

The door opened, and Lottie bounded in. "We came to find you! Your mom said you were changing into something special for the . . . oh!" She stopped short as she noticed Summer's dress and then snorted with laughter.

"I know! It's horrible, isn't it?" said Summer. "I look like a frilly fruit salad."

"It *does* look a bit like a fruit," Lottie said, chuckling. "I think it's all the green and orange."

Rosalind and Maya followed Lottie

inside, and they all stared at Summer's dress.

"That is *really* disgusting!" said Rosalind.

"Did you tell your mom that you don't like it?" asked Maya.

"I tried to," said Summer gloomily.

Just then, the queen of Mirrania came in. "Oh, you look lovely, Summer! That dress really suits you!" She paused. "But I'm afraid I've got some bad news. Mr. Fleck's discovered that his camera broke on the journey, and he needs to get it fixed. He can't take your picture until tomorrow. What a shame!"

Summer smiled. "Oh, that's OK! I don't mind!" She quickly pulled off the frilly dress, tossed it onto the bed, and put her other clothes back on again.

The queen frowned. "What's the matter? Don't you like the dress?"

"Well, um . . ." Summer hesitated. "It's just that I'd like to wear something more like this." She pointed at the simple red outfit she was wearing.

"Oh no, *that* would never work! You don't look royal enough. This photo is much too important for ordinary clothes." Her mom picked up the orange-and-green dress and hung it carefully inside Summer's wardrobe, smiling as she smoothed the ruffles. "I'll put this in here so it's ready for tomorrow."

When her mom left, Summer sat down on her bed and sighed.

"We'll help you wear what you want in the photo!" said Lottie firmly. "We just need to think of a plan."

"We could use ninja moves, just like we've done in our other Rescue Princess adventures," suggested Rosalind. "We could sneak outside with the frilly dress and hide it under a bush."

Summer managed a smile. "It's nice of you to offer, but I don't think we should."

Maya picked up Summer's small green jewelry box. She opened it and took out the necklace inside. "Wow! This is beautiful!"

A round jewel, filled with many colors, hung on the end of a gold chain. Red, blue, and green shone deep inside the heart of the gem, with specks of bright gold and dark purple.

"It's lovely, isn't it?" said Summer. "It's called an opal."

"It looks just like a rainbow!" said Lottie.

"That's what I call it — my Rainbow Opal," said Summer. "The best jewel-smiths in our kingdom made the necklace for me when I was born. Opals are a special jewel in Mirrania. Some people say that they were made when a rainbow touched the earth."

"It's so pretty!" Maya handed the necklace to Summer, who fastened it safely around her neck.

There was a tap on the window and a flash of bright wings, followed by a squawk.

Summer ran to the window and opened it carefully. "Hello, Kanga! Do you want us to come outside and play with you again?"

Kanga nudged Summer's hand fondly and squawked again.

"I think that means yes," said Lottie, grinning.

The four girls raced down the stairs and went right outside. Summer's rainbow necklace bounced as she ran. By the time they reached the gate that led to the woods, they were pink-cheeked and out of breath. Kanga, who had flown alongside them as they ran, landed on Summer's shoulder and folded his wings.

Summer closed the gate and breathed in the fresh forest smell. There were insects buzzing and swooping birdcalls in the treetops. The four girls went straight to the tree where they'd seen the koalas earlier.

"I can't see the koalas anymore," said Rosalind, staring at the tree with blue-gray leaves. "I wonder where they went."

"They probably climbed down and went up a different tree," said Summer. "I bet they're not far away."

They checked the trees nearby, but there was no sign of the koalas anywhere. Then a bush rustled near Rosalind's foot. "Oh,

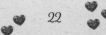

look!" she said. "There's the possum again."

A gray furry ear poked out from among the leaves.

Summer's eyes widened. "That's not a possum. That's the baby koala!"

CHAPTER THREE

The Koala That Got Left Behind

The bush shook again, and the baby koala looked out at them with frightened eyes.

"Is he there by himself?" said Lottie in surprise.

Rosalind knelt down and reached out her hand, but the little koala shrank back. "I think so. I can't see his mother."

"Do you think something bad has happened?" Maya twisted her braid worriedly.

"I don't know," said Summer, "but he

shouldn't be apart from his mom. He's much too young."

Lottie's green eyes lit up. "It'll be fine! He's got us — the Rescue Princesses — to help him! We can find his mom right away." Her tiara slipped sideways on her red curls, and she grabbed it before it fell off. "Maya, why don't you stay with the baby while the rest of us look for the mother?"

"We'll have to hurry," Summer told them. "My mom could call us in for lunch at any minute."

Maya crouched down and spoke soothingly to the baby, while the others spread out to search for the mother koala. Kanga flew from tree to tree as if he was helping them.

Summer pushed back her golden hair and scanned the treetops. It was really unusual to see a little koala without his mom. She couldn't help thinking that there must be a reason. Had the koalas been scared by the noisy motorcycle earlier? Maybe it had frightened them so much they'd wanted to hide.

"I can't see anything gray and furry in any of these trees," called Rosalind.

"I think I can see something," said Lottie.

Summer ran over and peered up at a dark lump near the top of a tree, almost hidden by leaves. "I'm not sure that's a koala. I'll go up and look." She swung herself easily onto a low branch and then pulled herself up the tree.

"Don't get too close and scare it," called Lottie.

Rosalind tutted. "Lottie! I'm sure she knows what to do!"

Summer held on to the trunk tightly as the wind swept through the branches, making the tree sway. "I can see it now. It's just part of the tree trunk and not an animal at all." She climbed down again.

In the distance, they heard the queen calling. "Girls! It's lunchtime!"

"But what about the baby koala?" said Maya. "We can't just leave him here."

The princesses gathered around the bush where the joey was hiding. He peered out at them, before sneezing quietly.

"Bless you!" cried Lottie. "Even his sneezes are cute!"

"I think we should take him with us," said Rosalind. "Then after lunch we'll search for his mom again."

"Let me pick him up," said Summer. "A wildlife expert once taught me how to hold a koala. I'll show you."

She tucked her rainbow opal necklace out of the way. Then she carefully leaned over the bush and picked up the little koala. She held him close to her shoulder, and his soft, furry ears tickled her chin. "Don't worry, little joey," she told him. "We'll take care of you."

Kanga flew down to a nearby tree and watched the princesses curiously. Then the girls heard the queen calling again. They hurried back toward the palace, leaving Kanga pecking at some fruit that he'd found dangling from a branch.

Luckily the king didn't mind having an extra furry guest at the dining table and told Summer that she could keep the little koala on her lap while she ate. The queen frowned a little, especially when the baby animal sneezed again.

"You must return him to his mother as soon as you can," said the king, looking at his daughter over the top of his glasses. "He's a wild animal, not a pet."

Summer put a strawberry-frosted cupcake on her plate. "Don't worry. We're going to look for her right after lunch."

She lifted the cupcake to her lips. Suddenly, the little koala leaned toward her hand and took a lick of frosting. Then he blinked and smacked his lips as if he wasn't quite sure he liked it.

"Hey!" said Summer. "That's my cupcake!"

The other princesses giggled, and the koala looked so funny licking his lips that Summer had to laugh, too.

"This is what happens when you have an animal at the table!" said the queen. "Finish quickly, please, Summer, and take him back outside where he belongs."

The king looked amused. "He's an inquisitive little thing! But koalas only eat eucalyptus leaves, so I don't think he really meant to steal your dessert."

After lunch, Summer carefully handed the koala to Maya because her arms were getting tired. The princesses thanked the king and queen for lunch and headed back outside.

"We should think of a name for him," said Maya, stroking the koala's furry coat.

"How about Fuzzy? Or Flumpy?" suggested Lottie.

"I think we should call him Cupcake," said Rosalind, grinning. "It was so funny when he took a taste of your frosting."

They all agreed that he should be Cupcake the koala from now on.

The princesses searched all afternoon for Cupcake's mother, looking up into every treetop and underneath every bush. Kanga came to watch them with his bright black eyes but didn't join in this time.

Each girl took a turn carrying Cupcake, who seemed much calmer now. While Lottie was holding him, he rested his head on her shoulder, closed his eyes, and went to sleep. The princesses continued searching. They saw plenty of possums, and a kangaroo leaping away into the distance, but there was no sign of the little koala's mother.

"We're getting nowhere. I'm really hot and thirsty, and there are scratches all over my legs from these spiky bushes." Rosalind rubbed her knees grumpily. "How big is this forest anyway?"

"It's really big. It stretches all the way to the nearest farm thirty miles away," said Summer. "I just didn't expect the mother koala to have gone very far."

The woods lay before them, just miles

of branches and leaves. Summer's heart sank, and she twisted her opal necklace. What were they going to do if they didn't find Cupcake's mother? He was too young to take care of himself.

"I think we should go back to the palace," said Rosalind.

"Let's search one more place," Summer said quickly. "The river's very close to here. Maybe that's where the mother koala went." She hurried down a slope, and the other girls followed her. Twigs crunched under their feet. Another possum poked his head out to investigate the noise.

They reached the river a few minutes later. It was a wide creek edged with trees whose branches dangled right over the blue-green water. The girls looked along the riverbank, and the baby koala woke up and gazed around, too.

"This is Rainbow Creek," said Summer. "The water's quite high because there's been a lot of rain lately."

"It's a rainbow river — like your rainbow necklace!" said Maya.

"Actually my opal was found here. It was picked up from the bottom of the river and made into a necklace." Summer held her opal up to the light, and all the colors sparkled.

"I still don't see the mother koala," said Rosalind with a sigh.

The princesses looked all around, but there was no sign of another koala. Cupcake squeaked unhappily and then sneezed.

"Poor Cupcake! You must be hungry by now," said Lottie, stroking his fur.

Cupcake sneezed again and started to shiver.

Maya looked alarmed. "He's not

hungry, Lottie. He's sick. Just look at how he's shivering!"

Summer's eyes widened. "You're right! He doesn't look well at all. Quick, we have to take him back to the palace!"

CHAPTER FOUR

The Flying Vet

The four princesses hurried back
through the trees and across the palace
lawn, with Lottie carrying Cupcake.
Kanga swooped over their heads and
landed in a tree near the palace door.
He watched the princesses run inside.

"Mom?" Summer yelled up the stairs.

The queen came down, her long purple
skirt brushing the steps as she walked.
"Summer! Please do *not* shout up the

stairs like that. If you need to speak to me, simply come and find me."

"Sorry!" Summer curtsied, hoping it would help. "It's just we're worried that the baby koala's sick." She gently lifted Cupcake out of Lottie's arms and showed him to the queen.

"Oh dear!" The queen looked closely at the little koala. "He certainly seems worse than he did at lunchtime. If he's sick, it would explain why he got separated from his mother. Maybe he felt too ill to hold on and that's why he got left behind."

Cupcake shivered again and clung to Summer's arm. She held him tightly.

"We'd better get someone to take a look at him." The queen paused at the bottom of the stairs. "Herbert!" she called loudly. "Could you come here a moment?"

Summer was pleased about getting help

for Cupcake, so she didn't point out that her mom had just shouted up the stairs, too!

The king appeared at the top. "Yes, my dear? Why are you calling?" He noticed the little koala. "Didn't you find the koala's mother, girls?"

"We looked for a long time, but we didn't see her anywhere," said Summer.

"And now we think Cupcake is sick," added Rosalind. "He keeps sneezing and shivering."

"Cupcake?" The king's eyebrows went up in surprise.

"That's what we've named him," explained Lottie.

"I think Cupcake needs some medicine," the queen told the king. "We should call for the flying vet."

♥

While the king rushed from room to room looking for the right telephone number,

Summer led the princesses to the kitchen. "Cupcake's still a baby, so he'll want milk," she said. "I just don't know how we should feed it to him."

"Do you need a bottle, Miss Summer?" asked the cook. "We used a bottle for that little kangaroo that fell out of its mother's pouch last year. It's in this cupboard." He took out the bottle and handed it to Rosalind, who filled it with milk.

"Summer?" said Lottie, frowning a little. "What's a *flying* vet?"

"Well, Mirrania is such a large country that it takes a long time to get around," explained Summer. "The nearest vet is probably miles away. So he'll fly here in a plane or a helicopter. I hope he can come right away."

Maya warmed the milk up and offered it to Cupcake, but he only took a few sips.

"Come on, Cupcake," she said. "This will help you feel better."

Cupcake gazed at her sadly and shivered.

"Let's go outside where we can keep a lookout for the vet," suggested Lottie.

They sat down on the palace steps, and Cupcake dozed on Summer's shoulder, only waking up to sneeze. A little while later, the girls heard a whirring noise in the distance.

"That sounds like a helicopter," said Rosalind.

The whirring grew into a deafening roar, and a green helicopter zoomed over the palace lawn like a gigantic bird. It lowered to the ground, sending swirls of dust into the air.

At last, a young woman with a dark ponytail climbed down and took off her helmet. She pulled a black bag out of the helicopter and hurried over to them.

Summer noticed a yellow badge pinned to her green T-shirt with the words *Forest Vets* printed on it.

"Hello, Princesses," she said quickly. "I'm Lizzie, and this must be the sick koala." She glanced at Cupcake. "Let's go inside so that I can look at him."

They went into the drawing room. The vet put down her bag and took Cupcake from Summer's arms. The girls watched as she checked his mouth and ears. Then she took a stethoscope out of her black bag and used it to listen to the little koala's heartbeat. At last, the vet sighed and shook her head.

"This isn't the kind of illness that's easy to cure, I'm afraid." She stroked Cupcake's head. "I can give you some drops to add to his milk. That might help him get stronger. But I don't have a medicine that will fix him right away."

Cupcake shivered, and Lottie took him from the vet and cuddled him.

"Thanks for coming to see him," said Summer, trying to hide her disappointment. She'd hoped the vet would make Cupcake better.

"You're welcome," said Lizzie, and she put a small bottle of yellow liquid down on the table. "I'll leave the drops here. Put three of them into each bottle of milk and try to get him to drink regularly."

"Thank you," said Maya, adding the drops to the bottle.

The vet frowned as she put her stethoscope away. "Before I go, I need to speak to your parents." She picked up her black bag and left.

Lottie held the milk bottle to Cupcake's mouth. "Come on, Cupcake. Drink some more," she coaxed. But the baby koala only took a few sips.

"I wish there was something else we could do to make him better," said Summer. "I thought the vet could do more to help."

Maya curled her braid around one finger. "I think she's more worried about him than she said."

"I think she gave up too easily," said Rosalind. "All she gave us is a tiny bottle of medicine."

"We'll just have to hope it works." Summer twisted her opal necklace in her hand. "I'm going to find a little blanket to wrap around Cupcake and then we can take turns holding him."

CHAPTER FIVE

The Story of the Opal

The princesses took good care of Cupcake. They fed him milk and put a small blanket around the little koala to keep him warm. Maya managed to get him to sleep again by gently stroking his fur.

After a while, they felt hungry, and the cook brought them plates of cookies and tall banana milk shakes. The cookies were made with deliciously big chocolate chips. It didn't take the princesses long to finish off every single one!

"There must be *something* that will make Cupcake better!" said Lottie, pacing up and down in front of the sofa.

"Shh! You'll wake him up," said Rosalind.

Before Lottie could reply, the queen came in. "Good news, Summer!" she said, smiling. "The photographer's back, and his camera is completely fixed. If you get changed quickly, he can take your picture before dinner."

Summer's face fell. "Oh! But we're looking after Cupcake right now, so maybe I should have my picture taken tomorrow."

"Don't be silly! You're not holding him at this exact moment, are you?" said the queen. "Quickly, now! Get changed into your new dress."

Summer took a deep breath. She would *have* to tell her mom how much she disliked that dress. But before she could decide what to say, the queen rushed off.

Annoyed, Summer went upstairs and changed into the frilly dress. As she put it on, she cheered herself up by inventing horrible names for the dress like *The Dress of Doom* and *The Ruffles of Terror*. She wondered if the whole kingdom would have nightmares about a giant fruit after seeing her photo. Then she went back downstairs, the dress scratching her legs with every step.

When she reached the drawing room, the queen was there with the other girls and Cupcake. Bill Fleck, the photographer, was staring around the room, holding the camera in one hand.

"Where *has* it gone?" asked Bill. "I'm sure I set it up in here. I just don't understand what happened."

"What's wrong?" asked Summer, trying to stand really straight so that the dress didn't rub against her legs.

"He lost his tripod," said Lottie, putting on a serious face. Then when Summer frowned, she added, "You know — the metal stand that the camera goes on."

"Oh!" Summer gazed around the room. There was a suspicious-looking shape behind the curtains. She looked at Lottie again and saw that her cheeks were pink and her mouth was shut tightly as if she was trying not to giggle. Maya and Rosalind were petting Cupcake, who sneezed again.

"Perhaps you left the camera stand in the car?" the queen suggested to Bill.

"That must be it!" He shook his head. "I'm just being forgetful. I'll go and get it."

The king came in. "Is everything all

right?" He caught sight of Summer and turned to the queen. "My dear, do you think it's the best idea to have Summer in a dress of that size and . . . er . . . magnificence for the photo? Surely she could wear something more ordinary."

Summer looked up hopefully. Maybe her mom would listen to her dad.

"That dress is perfect!" said the queen. "I'm determined that this will be the most elegant royal photo ever taken. We're almost ready now. I'll just see if Mr. Fleck needs any help." She followed the photographer out of the room.

The king sighed and scratched his head. Summer's shoulders drooped. Her mom was never going to change her mind.

Kanga flew in through the open window. Landing on the windowsill, he popped his head behind the curtain and croaked loudly.

"Shh! Don't give it away!" muttered Lottie.

The king looked at Summer over the top of his glasses and glanced at her necklace. "I'm glad you're wearing your rainbow necklace for the photo. I remember when that jewel was made for you when you were just a baby. There was a strange story about the opal."

Lottie jumped up, her eyes bright. "What was the story, Your Majesty? Please tell us!"

"I think I remember it," said Summer. "Was it something to do with the creek?"

Maya and Rosalind came closer to listen. Cupcake, who had been sleeping on Rosalind's shoulder, woke up and watched them all with big dark eyes.

"That's right, the story was about Rainbow Creek," said the king. "That was where the opal was found, of course. The jewel-smiths who crafted the necklace explained the story to me. They said that a wise, old man had taken the opal from the bottom of the river and he'd told them: *This rainbow jewel is a gift from the sky. Its healing powers will be released when it's dipped back into the waters it came from."*

There was a moment of silence.

"So you see, like all the best jewels, it's not just something pretty to look at," added the king.

Summer bit her lip. An idea was starting to grow inside her head. She looked over at Cupcake, who was shivering in Rosalind's arms.

The queen rushed back in, followed by Bill Fleck. "It is most incomprehensible!" she sighed, straightening her crown. "If you brought the camera stand in, then it should be right here! Oh, I *do* want that picture taken today!"

"Come, my dear!" The king took the queen's hand. "Let's go and get a nice cup of tea and leave Mr. Fleck to find the stand. I'm sure it will turn up."

"I'll check all the other downstairs rooms," said Bill Fleck. "I bet I left it somewhere by mistake."

As soon as everyone had gone, Summer turned to the others with her blue eyes shining. "I should have thought of it before! Now I know what we can do!"

"What do you mean?" asked Maya.

"We can take my opal to Rainbow Creek." Summer held up her colorful necklace. Kanga flew down to her shoulder and tilted his head to stare at the jewel.

"You're talking about your dad's story, aren't you?" said Rosalind. "If the opal really has healing powers, then that could help Cupcake."

"Exactly!" Summer smiled. "And we know that jewels can be magical, so maybe the story is true!"

"We need to dip the opal into the river just like the wise, old man told the jewel-smiths," said Maya.

"We'd better hurry," said Lottie urgently. "If we don't go before the photographer gets back, we'll miss our chance."

Squawk! Kanga fluttered toward the door before returning to perch on Summer's shoulder. There was a noise in the hallway.

"What is it, Kanga?" said Summer.

Lottie ran to the door and peeked around. "Your mom's coming back. We need a way out of here!"

Rosalind clutched Cupcake tightly and whispered, "All we have to do is climb out the window. It's one of the simplest ninja moves there is!"

Summer ran to the window and opened it wider. Kanga flew out and soared into the cloudy sky. Lottie and Maya climbed out first. Then Rosalind handed Cupcake to Maya, before scrambling over the windowsill.

Summer remembered the hidden tripod and pulled it out from behind the curtain. She put it on the floor near the sofa. It would seem as if it had been lying there unnoticed all the time.

Her heart raced as she heard her mom's voice right outside the door. She hopped out the window, nearly getting her legs tangled in her long, frilly dress. Rosalind pulled her down onto the grass.

"Stay low!" hissed Rosalind. "We *have to* get away without being seen!"

CHAPTER SIX

Thunderclouds

Summer crouched on the ground below
the window with Rosalind next to her.
She tried to stay still, even though the
ground felt really hard and her dress was
making her legs itch. Any noise might
draw her mom to the window. From the
corner of her eye, she could see Lottie and
Maya hiding around the corner of the
house with Cupcake.

"That's strange! Where have the girls

gone?" The queen's voice drifted through the open window.

"There's my tripod!" said Bill Fleck. "It must have been here the whole time."

"Here's your cup of tea, my dear," said the king. "I'm sure the princesses will be back in a moment." There was the sound of a teaspoon clinking against a teacup.

Summer lifted her head to look over the windowsill. The king and queen were sitting on the sofa, and Bill was setting up the camera. None of them were looking toward the window.

"That poor little koala!" The queen sighed. "Do you think we should tell Summer what the vet said before she left?"

Summer froze. What was her mom talking about?

"I could see that the little creature's not doing well, Your Majesty," said Bill Fleck. "But surely he'll get better?"

"I'm afraid he might get worse," replied the queen. "The vet said he's terribly sick. If he hasn't improved by the end of today, he'll probably get weaker and weaker. I just hope he pulls through."

Summer's heart filled with sadness. She couldn't let Cupcake get worse. He *had* to start getting better — he just had to!

She looked at Rosalind, who nodded. Slowly they crawled away from the window, keeping their heads low. They scrambled up as soon as they were out of sight and ran to the corner where Lottie and Maya were waiting. Black clouds gathered overhead, and rain began to fall.

Summer stroked Cupcake's fur, and he looked at her sadly and whimpered.

"What's wrong?" Maya asked her. "You look really serious."

"The vet didn't tell us how sick he really is," said Summer, and she told the others what she'd overheard. "We have to use the rainbow opal right now," she added. "We have to help him before he gets any worse."

"We're Rescue Princesses," said Lottie firmly. "We'll help him no matter how hard it is."

A flash of lightning lit the sky as the princesses crossed the palace lawn. Then the thunder growled, and the rain grew heavier. It pattered down on their heads, making their tiaras slippery on their wet hair.

Once they'd gone through the gate, Lottie beckoned them to join her underneath a tree. "Let's stop under here for a minute," she called over the drumming noise of the rain. "When the rain gets lighter, we can keep going."

The rain shower grew heavier until every dip in the ground became a puddle. At last it slowed down, and the girls made their way toward the river. Kanga flew from tree to tree in front of them, the rainwater sparkling on his bright feathers.

"How will the magic inside the opal work?" asked Maya, trying not to slip on the muddy ground. Cupcake clung tight to her shoulder.

"I don't really know," said Summer. "What do you think, Rosalind? You're good at getting magical jewels to work, aren't you?"

"Sometimes." Rosalind frowned. "But I've never done anything with an opal before."

The thunder rumbled over their heads again.

Maya looked at the sky. "I hope there won't be another big downpour."

The sun began to set, and the woods grew darker. The princesses scrambled down the slope until they reached Rainbow Creek at the bottom of the valley. The river was flowing fast, full of extra water from the rainstorm. Summer unhooked her necklace and made her way gingerly down the bank. She skidded on the wet earth and grabbed hold of a bush to steady herself.

The ruffles on her dress got caught on a bramble. She pulled at the frilly stuff, not caring when it made a loud ripping sound. The rest of her dress was splattered with mud, which had left a splotchy brown pattern across the green and orange stripes.

"Go on, Summer! Just dip the jewel in the water like the wise man said in the

story," said Lottie. "I bet something will happen right away."

Summer held out the necklace and leaned over the water. She caught her breath. Would the magic begin at once? Did she need to dip the rainbow opal in the river for very long? She wasn't really sure. She would just have to try it and see what happened.

The opal glowed as it dangled above the surging river. The last rays of the setting sun broke through the gray clouds, making the rainbow colors shine inside the jewel. Then the clouds blocked out the sun again, and the wind grew stronger. The tree's branches trembled overhead.

The wind gave a sudden gust, and Kanga, who was perching nearby, squawked in alarm. Summer was knocked sideways by the wind. She stumbled, dropping the necklace.

"Oh no!" she cried. "Come back!" She crouched on the riverbank and thrust her arm into the swirling water. But her hand came out empty.

Lottie and Rosalind ran to her side. "Careful! Don't fall in," said Rosalind. "Rivers can be dangerous, especially after a storm."

"But I dropped the jewel!" said Summer, tears coming to her eyes. "The wind pushed me over and now the rainbow opal is gone!"

"What bad luck," said Lottie. "I can't see the jewel at all. I thought something would change when it went under the water."

The three girls stared at the place where the necklace had sunk but nothing happened.

Maya called to them from the top of the bank. "Cupcake seems cold, and he's

shivering more than ever." She hugged
the little koala. "I wish we hadn't brought
him outside. I think we should go back."

Summer climbed miserably back up
the riverbank. She hoped the rainbow
opal wasn't their only chance of helping
Cupcake. The jewel had probably sunk
to the bottom of the river, and it was all
her fault.

CHAPTER SEVEN

The Ruined Dress

Another rain shower started as the princesses walked back to the palace. Rain trickled off their dresses, and their shoes squelched with water. Cupcake sneezed and clung tightly to Maya.

The queen met them at the front door, and her eyes widened in horror. "Oh my goodness, look at you! Come inside quickly."

The girls ran in and dripped water onto the palace floor.

"Summer, what on earth have you been doing?" cried the queen. "Just look at your new dress! I expected you to be more careful — you know I wanted you to wear that outfit for the photo."

Summer's dress was a patchwork of mud stains. A large rip ran across the material, and one of the ruffles was hanging on by a thread.

"I'm sorry, Mom. It got caught on a bramble," said Summer, too worried about Cupcake to feel glad about the ruined dress.

The queen shook her head and muttered something about stain treatments. Then she sent one of the maids to collect towels and told the king to get a fire going in the drawing room.

Kanga gave a low squawk and hopped along the bannister. Then he shook rainwater off his wings. Cupcake let out a little whimper.

"The poor animal," said the queen. "Give him to me, and I'll dry him." She took Cupcake and wrapped him up in a towel. Then she sent the princesses upstairs to get dry and change into warm pajamas. "Don't forget to dry your hair!" she called after them.

By the time the girls came back down, a fire was burning brightly in the fireplace and Cupcake had gone to sleep inside his towel.

The princesses sat down on the sofa in their fluffy pajamas and ate delicious tomato soup with warm buttered rolls.

The queen fussed over them. "Eat up now! You need some good hot food after getting soaked like that. I know you wanted to find the koala's mother but going out in the rain was just silly!"

Summer didn't want to mention the rainbow opal, and she shot a warning look at the others so that they didn't say anything. "I'm sorry!" she told her mom. "The soup tastes great. Can we have some more?"

After dinner, Lottie made a fresh bottle of milk for Cupcake and put some drops of medicine into it. Summer gently pressed the bottle to the baby koala's mouth. He only drank a little and gazed at her with big dark eyes.

"Please get better," she whispered, stroking the pale fur on his stomach.

Cupcake squeaked. Summer was worried about how quiet and still he'd become. She took him to her room that night, and he settled down on her pillow. She watched him for a while before going to sleep, wondering what she was going to do.

Summer woke up in the middle of the night. Her bed was shaking slightly. Sleepily, she switched on the light and found that Rosalind was sitting on the end of the bed.

"Hello." Rosalind had a serious look in her blue eyes. "I need to talk to you."

"Huh? What time is it?" Summer sat up in bed. Cupcake woke up, too, and shivered.

"It's nearly midnight." Rosalind walked over to Summer's window and pulled the curtains open. "And it's stopped raining."

A bright crescent moon shone in the cloudless night sky.

"But it's still dark." Summer rubbed her eyes. "Why are we talking about the rain in the middle of the night?"

"I couldn't get to sleep," said Rosalind. "And then I started thinking . . . what if

the opal's magic is the kind of thing that takes time? What if we left the river before it even started? What if it's down there under the water working right now?"

"I hadn't thought of that." Summer felt a fluttering in her stomach. "Rosalind! You're a genius!"

"Well, we don't know if I'm right yet or even if we'll be able to find the opal," said Rosalind. "But I think we should go down there and look."

The bedroom door creaked open, letting in a rectangle of light from the hallway. "You guys *do* know you're talking really loudly, right?" said Lottie.

Rosalind explained her plan to Lottie, and then they had to wake up Maya and explain it all over again.

"So we should definitely try to find the rainbow opal right now," Lottie finished. "In fact, there's only one problem."

"What's that?" asked Rosalind.

"If we find the rainbow opal, how do we get it out of the water?" said Lottie. "The river's too fast and too deep for any of us to go in."

"Do you have a fishing net, Summer?" asked Maya. "A small one that's like a stick with a net on the end."

"No, I don't." Summer picked up Cupcake and hugged him. "I *wish* there was a way to reach it. . . ." An idea popped into her head. "Wait a second! The ruffles on that awful dress are just like a net. That's why the dress is so itchy!"

Maya ran to Summer's bedroom and brought back the dress. "You're right — these frilly pieces are the same material as a net. We just need to cut them off and sew them together. Are you sure your mom won't mind?"

Summer shrugged. "I don't like the dress, and it's ruined already. At least this way we can do something useful with it."

Maya and Lottie got to work, quickly cutting the scratchy ruffles off the dress and sewing them together. Finally, after a lot of thought, Rosalind stuck four rulers together with sticky tape to make the handle part of the fishing net.

"It looks a little strange," said Rosalind, picking up the net and turning it around.

"I'm sure it'll work," Lottie told her.

"One of us has to stay here with Cupcake," said Maya. "He shouldn't go out into the cold night air. I'll stay if you want."

"Thanks, Maya," said Summer gratefully.

Maya sat down on the bed next to Cupcake, who was leaning against the pillow with his eyes shut. He didn't open them when Maya picked him up. She stroked his fur, her forehead creasing. "His breathing is very slow," she said anxiously.

The other princesses watched, waiting to see whether Cupcake would wake up. But he didn't.

Maya looked at his still face and swallowed. "You'd better go and find that rainbow opal. And hurry!"

CHAPTER EIGHT

Rainbow Creek at Midnight

Summer, Lottie, and Rosalind crept downstairs, found their shoes, and slipped out the front door. Then Lottie switched on the flashlight that she'd brought and lit their way across the palace lawn. Their pajama legs brushed against the wet grass. Rosalind carried the homemade fishing net.

Summer stopped at the gate and looked back at the palace. There was a faint light at her bedroom window. Maya would be inside, looking after Cupcake. Her throat tightened. She'd never seen an animal look so sick.

Lottie opened the gate. "We got out without anyone hearing us. Now we just have to find that opal!"

"Let's just hope we can reach the jewel with the fishing net," said Rosalind.

The forest felt different in the dark. Fluttering sounds came from overhead, and Summer couldn't tell if it was a night bird or just the wind in the trees. There was a scuffling on the ground, and a pair of little yellow eyes blinked at them for a moment, then they were gone.

"Should I go first?" asked Summer. "I know the way to the river really well."

"OK, lead the way." Lottie handed her the flashlight, and they went through the trees, one behind the other.

They heard the roaring of the river

before they could see it. Summer knew from the noise that the creek was still swollen with rain from the storm.

Slithering down the bank, she searched for the place where she'd stood that afternoon — the place where she'd dropped the necklace.

Then she saw footprints in the mud. Yes, this was where they'd been. She remembered the trees opposite and the shape of the bank. She shone the flashlight at the water. "I can't see anything. Maybe the necklace was washed along before it sank."

"But it looked like it sank right away," said Rosalind.

Summer frowned. "I thought it did, too, but the river's flowing so fast right now. I think it may have gotten pushed along."

The girls scrambled through the woods, following the flow of the river. In many places, the trees grew right down to the edge of the water, making it hard to walk along the bank.

"These silly branches are in the way!" said Lottie, pushing them aside roughly.

"Hey! You're making them flip back at me!" said Rosalind.

"I didn't mean to," began Lottie. "It's just —"

"Wait! What's that?" Rosalind pointed at the other side of the river.

"It's the moonlight shining on the water," said Lottie.

Summer peered across the river, and her heart skipped. There was a dot of white light in the water, close to the opposite bank. As they watched, it flickered and changed to a warm gold, then it became a cool, icy green.

"That *isn't* just the moonlight!" breathed Summer. "That's magic!"

"But is it the rainbow opal?" said Rosalind. "It's hard to see!"

The girls got as close to the water's edge as they could, and Summer shone the flashlight across the river.

"Those colors are amazing! It must be the opal." Summer watched the light change from a dazzling blue to a deep fiery red.

"I think I can see the chain of the necklace," said Lottie. "Look!" She took the flashlight from Summer and shone the beam upward a little. There, caught on a low-hanging branch just above the water, was the glittering gold chain.

"We won't be able to reach it with this." Rosalind held up the fishing net. "The river's too wide. How can we get over to the other side, Summer? Is there a bridge?"

Summer bit her lip. "There is. But it's

farther along the river, and it would take us too long to find it."

"Maybe we could use a boat," suggested Lottie.

"The river current's really strong," said Summer. "We'd float away down the river as soon as we pushed off." She frowned, thinking hard. "There *must* be a way to get over!"

"Stilts?" suggested Lottie, her eyes gleaming. "Or we could make our own rope bridge?"

"Rope! I tied some rope to a tree near here a few days ago," said Summer. "I was using it as a swing."

Taking the flashlight back from Lottie, she scrambled up the bank and searched the trees. She'd chosen a tall one with sturdy branches to hang the rope on. It dangled there, swaying slightly in the wind.

"I don't think a rope bridge will work," she told the others. "But maybe one of us could swing across on the rope."

"Great idea! We need to tie it to a tree right next to the creek," said Rosalind.

Summer handed Lottie the flashlight and climbed quickly up the tree. She sat with her legs dangling on either side of the branch, struggling to undo the rope knot. "I tied it really tight so that it didn't slip off while I was swinging," she called down to the others.

At last, the knot came undone, and Summer let the rope drop to the ground before climbing back down the tree trunk.

"Here's a good tree," Rosalind called from the edge of the riverbank. "It's got really flat branches, and it looks like it's strong."

Lottie and Summer ran to join her, and Lottie shone the flashlight up at the tree.

"That's great!" Summer climbed up and tied the rope firmly to the branch. "Pull on it — see if I've tied the knot tight enough."

Rosalind pulled the rope, then she tried dangling from it with the fishing net in one hand. "It feels strong to me. So who's going to swing over?"

Summer climbed back down, and the three girls exchanged looks.

"I don't mind swinging across . . ." began Summer.

"No, it can't be you," said Lottie firmly. "Whoever goes across will be stuck there. They'll have to walk along to the bridge to get back. We need you here so that you can find a quick way back through the woods to the palace. You're the one that knows the way. Cupcake's life could depend on it."

"So will you swing over?" asked Summer.

Lottie nodded. "I'll do it."

"Hold on a minute," said Rosalind. "If you swing across and then you're stuck on the other side, how do we get the rainbow opal back to Cupcake?"

"I'll throw it across to you," said Lottie.

"But if it drops in the river, we'll be right back where we started," said Rosalind.

"Don't worry — I have an idea." Summer turned away from the river and cupped her hands around her mouth. "Kanga? Can you hear me?"

There was a long silence. Then they heard the whirr of wings, and there was a flash of blue-and-yellow feathers in the darkness.

CHAPTER NINE

The Magic Inside the Rainbow

Kanga landed on Summer's shoulder, and she patted his wings. "Good boy, Kanga! I know you don't like flying in the dark." She turned to Lottie. "When you get to the necklace, I'll send Kanga across. He'll grab it from you and bring it back to us. Here, take the flashlight. You'll need it to find your way to the bridge."

"Thanks!" Lottie put the flashlight in her pajama pocket. Then she grabbed the rope and climbed to the top of the bank. "Watch out, everyone! I'm going to swing."

"Wait!" Rosalind hurried over and gave her the homemade fishing net. "Take this as well! You might need it to reach the necklace."

Lottie held the net in one hand and the rope in the other, and took an enormous leap off the top of the riverbank. She swung across the fast-flowing river, her feet skimming over the water.

Summer held her breath, hoping that the rope would take Lottie all the way across. But the other girl gave a shriek, and there was a splash as she landed in the water near the opposite bank. She jumped up and waved to them, only up to her ankles in water. "It's all right!" she called to them. "This part is shallow. I'll be able to get the necklace easily."

She waded toward the glowing light made by the opal, but the river became deeper, and she had to climb back onto the bank.

Summer and Rosalind watched anxiously. "Try using the net!" shouted Rosalind.

Lottie crouched down and stretched the fishing net toward the necklace. She dipped the net into the water to scoop out the opal and then jiggled the branch where the chain was caught. At last, the necklace fell into the net, caught by the frilly material.

"She did it!" cried Summer, and Kanga gave a happy squawk.

Lottie pulled the necklace out of the net and held it up to show them. The rainbow opal dangled on the end of the chain and its ever-changing colors glowed brightly in the dark.

"Now, Kanga," said Summer urgently. "Could you please fly over and bring the necklace back to us?"

Kanga flew over to Lottie and took the necklace chain in his beak. Then he hopped onto her arm and spread his wings to fly back again.

"He understood you," said Rosalind, amazed.

Summer smiled. "He's always been a very clever bird."

The rainbow opal shone as Kanga swooped back across the river. He dropped the jewel into Summer's hand and settled on a tree branch.

"Thank you, Kanga!" said Summer, beaming. "Lottie! You need to go that way to get to the bridge." She pointed up the river. "You won't get lost if you follow the creek."

"Don't worry, I have the flashlight, so

I'll be fine. I'll meet you back at the palace," called Lottie.

Summer climbed up the riverbank, holding the bright opal in the palm of her hand. The jewel shone with a warm orange light and then flickered and turned to a deep, mysterious purple.

Rosalind clambered up behind her. "That jewel's amazing!" She watched as it changed color. "It shines much brighter than the jewels in our rings. That must mean the magic inside is really strong."

"I hope so." Summer thought of poor Cupcake. Everything depended on the jewel being able to help him. Reaching the top of the bank, she started to run.

The two girls raced through the trees together. The leaves and branches glowed with the light from the jewel. Summer thought how strange it was to see the woods lit up by one color after another.

It felt as if they were running through an enchanted forest.

She stopped at the back gate and fumbled with the catch. Rosalind looked up at the palace and noticed an anxious face at Summer's bedroom window. "There's Maya!" she said, pointing.

Maya waved frantically at them before disappearing.

A cold feeling spread through Summer's insides. "She's trying to send us a message. Something must be wrong!"

They dashed across the lawn into the palace and ran up the dark stairs. Summer opened her bedroom door and her chest tightened. She tried to get her breath back so that she could speak. "How . . . how is he, Maya?"

"He got worse after you left." Maya held the little koala very tightly and her dark eyes were sad. "I tried to get him to drink

some more milk from the bottle, but he wouldn't."

Summer stroked Cupcake's fluffy stomach. She felt his chest rise and fall very slightly as he breathed. His head rested on Maya's arm.

"But you found the rainbow opal," said Maya. "So everything will be all right, won't it?"

Summer opened her hand to reveal the opal necklace, and rainbow light burst across the dark room. "I hope so. It's just that my dad's story didn't tell us how the healing powers work or what we have to do."

"Try hanging it around his neck," said Rosalind.

Summer carefully looped the chain of the necklace over Cupcake's head. The chain was way too long for him. It dangled down so that the shining opal lay against his little legs.

The princesses waited, hardly daring to breathe as they watched the jewel. Kanga watched, too. The opal turned a deep sapphire blue, then changed to pale yellow.

"Amazing!" whispered Maya. "All the colors of the rainbow one by one."

Cupcake's nose twitched, and he whimpered.

Rosalind frowned. "Nothing's happening! Why isn't it working?"

"Maybe we just need to wait," said Summer anxiously. "Maybe it takes time for the opal to make him better."

The minutes ticked by. Kanga stayed quiet, watching with beady eyes. Maya sat down on the bed with Cupcake on her lap. Summer knelt down next to her, staring at the baby koala and hoping for a sign that he felt well again. Cupcake closed his eyes, and his head flopped against Maya's arm.

"This is no good," said Rosalind at last. "We must have done something wrong."

Summer pushed her hand through her golden hair. "But how? I just don't know what else to do!" She picked up the opal and held it closer to the little koala's chest.

Cupcake opened his little eyes wide and watched the jewel change color.

"Please get better, Cupcake!" said Maya softly.

Cupcake gazed steadily at the rainbow opal. Then suddenly he leaned forward and licked it.

Summer gasped. "Cupcake! You funny little thing!"

CHAPTER TEN

The Perfect Photo

Soon after Cupcake licked the rainbow opal, its glowing light began to fade. It grew dimmer and dimmer until it looked just like an ordinary opal again.

Cupcake seemed to have more energy. He lifted his head off Maya's arm and looked around. Then he wriggled and wriggled. Rosalind tried to give him the bottle of milk, and he drank the whole thing! The girls grinned at one another. Kanga squawked and hopped up and down on the windowsill.

Summer undid the necklace from Cupcake's neck and put it back around her own. "It looks like the magic of the opal worked after all!" She kissed the top of Cupcake's furry head.

"But who would have guessed he needed to lick it?" said Rosalind. "Lottie is never going to believe it!"

The door burst open, and Lottie staggered in with the flashlight in her hand. Her pajamas were covered in smears of mud, and there were leaves in her hair.

"Lottie!" said Summer. "Great job finding your way back over the bridge."

"I'm so tired," Lottie panted. "How's Cupcake?"

"He's much better now," said Maya,

smiling. "The rainbow jewel was amazing!"

They told Lottie everything that had happened. Then, because they all felt very sleepy after the night's adventures, they settled down to rest for a few minutes. Maya and Summer lay across Summer's bed, while Rosalind curled up on the soft rug and Lottie lay back in an armchair. Kanga fluffed up his feathers and tucked his beak under his wing.

When they opened their eyes again, sunlight was pouring through the curtains. Maya's mom stood in the doorway looking at them all.

"Well, I didn't expect to find you all asleep together! I hope you didn't stay up too late," said the queen. "How's the little koala this morning?"

Summer picked up Cupcake and gave

him a hug. "He seems much hungrier, and I think that's a good sign."

"That *is* a good sign," said her mom. "That medicine the vet gave us must have done the trick." She smiled.

Lottie's stomach rumbled. "Actually, I'm pretty hungry, too!"

"Breakfast will be ready very soon," said the queen, smiling. "There'll be toast, fried eggs, and bacon."

"Mmm!" Lottie's eyes grew round. "I'm going to get dressed!"

After a hearty breakfast, the princesses took Cupcake outside. They sat on the palace steps and took turns feeding him a bottle of milk.

The king came outside, too, and looked at them thoughtfully over the top of his glasses. "You've done a great job looking after that little koala. It seems like the medicine was more useful than we thought."

"Yes, it must have been," replied Summer, her cheeks growing pink. Would her dad believe her if she told him about the opal's magic? He smiled at her and winked. Her dad probably would believe her, Summer decided. But for now the magical opal was a Rescue Princesses' secret!

Cupcake finished his milk, and Summer was just about to suggest that they go down to the woods, when she heard her mom calling.

"Summer! Time for your photo!" said the queen.

"Rats!" said Summer. "I'd forgotten about that."

"But at least you don't have to wear that awful dress," said Lottie. "The frilly piece got turned into our fishing net."

"That's true!" said Summer. "I hope my mom will let me wear something nicer."

💜

Summer hurried into the drawing room wearing her favorite red dress and a tiara that was sprinkled with little flowers. The other girls had also gotten dressed. Rosalind came in behind her in a dark blue dress and a crown made from gold and sapphires. Maya paused in the doorway, trying to straighten her heart-shaped tiara on top of her black hair.

"Here you go, Maya," said Lottie, helping her. Her own gold-and-ruby tiara was completely crooked and her red dress had some mud on the sleeves, but that didn't worry her at all!

The queen was waiting for them. "Girls, you all look lovely!" she said. "I wonder if you'd like to be in the royal photo with Summer?"

"Oh yes!" said Summer. "*Please* be in the photo! I don't want to have my picture taken on my own."

"I don't mind!" said Rosalind. "I like having my picture taken."

"I don't mind, either," said Maya.

Lottie grinned. "Does that mean our picture will be on TV? I've never been on TV before."

The king came in and heard Lottie's remark. He smiled. "The picture will be shown to the whole kingdom. You'll be famous throughout the land."

"Maybe we should brush your hair a little first," murmured the queen, using the hairbrush on each princess.

Summer set Cupcake down carefully on one of the sofa cushions. He'd fallen asleep again, and she didn't want him disturbed by the clicking of the camera.

"Is everyone ready?" said Bill Fleck, looking through the camera lens. "Big smiles, everybody!"

Squawk! Kanga flew into the room and perched on Summer's shoulder.

"Oh dear!" The queen flapped her hands at Kanga. "Shoo, shoo! We can't have a parrot in a royal photo."

"Oh, please, Mom!" cried Summer. "Kanga's really clean and tidy."

"You won't look fancy enough if we let a bird into the picture," said the queen, and Kanga flapped his wings indignantly.

"If I may, Your Majesty, the parrot's feathers make a nice color contrast," said Bill earnestly. "I think you will be pleased with the result."

"Please, Mom! I don't want to look fancy, I just want to look like me," Summer pleaded. "I'll help with the dishes for weeks!"

The king's eyes twinkled. "I think the people of Mirrania will be happy to see that they have an animal-loving princess."

The queen sighed. "Oh, all right, then."

Summer's heart lifted. She smoothed her dress and straightened her rainbow opal necklace. This was better than she'd ever hoped for — a royal photo with her friends and Kanga!

The girls all smiled as Bill focused his camera. "Ready? Say cheese!"

CHAPTER ELEVEN

The Royal Academy for Princesses

Later that day, the four princesses sat on the sofa in the palace drawing room and waited for the royal photo to be shown on TV. The king and queen were sitting in armchairs, drinking cups of tea. Kanga hopped up and down on the back of the sofa. Summer was hugging Cupcake, who had just finished another bottle of milk.

"I hope my eyes aren't closed," said Maya. "I usually blink when anyone takes my picture."

"I can promise you that you all look lovely," said the queen, smiling fondly. "The king and I checked the picture before we gave it to the TV station, so there's nothing to worry about."

A picture of the four girls and Kanga flashed onto the television screen. In the photo, the princesses had big smiles while Kanga tilted his head and lifted one wing, as if to wave.

"There it is!" cried Lottie, leaping up from the sofa.

The newscaster on the television began to speak. "And now, we're pleased to show you the royal photo of Princess Summer. The whole kingdom has been eagerly waiting to see this picture since the princess's tenth birthday. Summer is pictured here with her friends, Princesses Maya, Lottie, and Rosalind, and her much-loved parrot, Kanga."

Kanga squawked.

"We all look great," said Rosalind, smoothing her hair.

"I'm so glad I didn't blink at the wrong time," said Maya.

The newscaster continued. "The king and queen have also announced that Summer will be attending the Royal Academy for Princesses in the kingdom of Middingland once the new year begins. We'd like to wish Summer the best of luck as she starts Princess School. And now on to more news . . ."

The king switched off the television. There was a moment of silence. The king and queen looked at Summer. Lottie, Maya, and Rosalind stared at the king and queen. Summer gazed at the blank TV screen, and Cupcake was quiet, too. Only Kanga continued as normal, hopping up and down and pecking at the sofa.

"Erm . . . we have something we need to talk to you about," the king told Summer. "We didn't know they were going to announce it like that on television. But never mind! We've decided to send you to the Royal Academy for Princesses next semester. It's an excellent royal school!"

"But I don't want to go to this academy place!" Summer's face turned pink.

"Please come!" said Lottie excitedly. "I'm going there, too! My older sister, Emily, goes there already, and she says it's really fun."

"Really?" said Summer.

"She loves it there!" said Lottie. "It's in Middingland, which is where we come from, but there are princesses from all around the world at the school. And they let you keep a pet!"

Summer glanced at Kanga, who was

busily preening his feathers. "Are you really happy about going there?"

Lottie nodded. "I'm starting next semester. I can't wait! They have bunk beds, and the academy's by the sea, so you get to go swimming and sailing."

"Let's talk about it after dinner when you've had time to get used to the idea," said the queen.

"All right," said Summer. Cupcake wriggled in her arms, and she kissed the top of his furry head. "I think Cupcake's strong enough to go back to the forest."

"We should go and see if his mother's come back for him," said Rosalind. "She could be looking for him right now."

The princesses went outside, and Kanga flew over their heads.

"What are we going to do about being Rescue Princesses if two of us are at school?" said Maya suddenly. "We won't be able to keep helping animals."

"I've been thinking about that," said Lottie. "I think we *can* keep being Rescue Princesses, but we might need more girls to join us. Imagine a whole school full of princesses who all know how to rescue animals!"

"I'm going to ask my mom and dad if I can come to the Royal Academy, too," said Rosalind. "It sounds really fun."

Lottie opened the gate, and they walked into the woods together. The birds chattered in the treetops, and the bushes nearby rustled.

"I know that Cupcake's home is here in the woods, but I wish we could keep him forever." Maya sighed.

"Me too!" said Lottie. "I know he belongs with his mother, but he's been so adorable." She rubbed her cheek against Cupcake's furry ear.

A loud rustling sound at the top of a tree made them look up, and a large koala climbed down the trunk.

"Is that Cupcake's mother?" said Rosalind.

"I think so." Summer set Cupcake carefully down on the grass. "If it is, then they'll know each other right away."

The girls backed away a little so that they didn't alarm the animals. Then they watched as the large koala reached the ground and bounded straight over to the baby. The koalas sniffed each other for a moment. Then Cupcake climbed onto his mother's back, and she clambered up the tree again.

Cupcake clung on to his mother and gazed at Summer with big dark eyes.

Summer called up to him. "Take care, Cupcake! I won't forget you."

With a flash of bright feathers, Kanga flew down to Summer's shoulder and chattered into her ear.

Summer laughed. "Don't worry, Kanga! I won't forget you, either."

"We could never forget *you*, Kanga," said Lottie. "You're the only parrot I've ever met who hops like a kangaroo!"

Can't wait for
the Rescue Princesses' next
daring animal adventure?

The Golden Shell

Turn the page for
a sneak peek!

First Day of School

Princess Ella gazed at the trees and hedges flashing past the car window. She linked her fingers together tightly and tried to ignore the fluttering feeling inside her. It wouldn't be long now. Soon they would reach the Royal Academy for Princesses, her new school!

She tucked her wavy dark hair behind her tiara and smoothed the gray pleats of her new school skirt. She was trying not to think about missing home, especially her puppy, Sesame, with his beautiful brown eyes and soft little paws. But thinking about her new school didn't make her feel better, either. Her mom had told her that the school was enormous. What if she got lost trying to find her way around? What if none of the other girls wanted to talk to her? What if —

"Are you all right, Ella?" Her mom, Queen Jade, suddenly leaned toward her. "You look a little pale. Do you feel sick?"

"No, I'm fine." Ella tried to smile.

"Really?" The queen frowned. "You don't look fine. Maybe we'd better stop for a minute." She leaned forward to speak to the royal driver. "Stop at the side of the road, please."

The car drew to a stop next to a hedge. Ella's dad, King George, quietly snored from the front passenger seat.

"Your father's nodded off again," said the queen, opening the car door. "Out you go! You'll feel much better after some fresh air."

Ella climbed out onto a grassy area dotted with purple flowers. They were in a narrow lane with tall hedges on both sides. The sun shone brightly, and thin wisps of white clouds floated in the sky.

The queen climbed out of the car, holding on to her golden crown. "Ah, there's something wonderful about the air here!" she said, smiling. "It makes me feel energetic! I remember when I used to come to school here, many years ago. One day, we all went on a long walk through the fields and . . ." The queen continued talking, but Ella didn't listen closely to the rest.

Her mom had been talking about the old days at school a lot. She'd talked about it while making Ella try on her new green-and-gray uniform. Then she'd talked some more while packing Ella's suitcase. Ella knew that her mom had loved going to the Royal Academy for Princesses. She just wasn't sure she was going to like it, too.

She breathed in deeply. Her mom was right. The air did seem fresher here. She noticed a gap in the hedge a little farther along and went to look through it. Sheep were grazing in the field on the other side. Ella stared at the view beyond the field, and her heart beat faster. In the distance, there was a towering red-stone castle and a sparkling blue sea.

"Wow! That's a really big castle." Ella gazed at its square turrets. It looked much more old-fashioned than their palace back home.

"There it is!" said her mom, joining her.

"Harebell Castle — home to the Royal Academy for Princesses."

"That's Harebell Castle? I didn't know we were so close!" said Ella, surprised.

"Yes, we're almost there." The queen smiled. "Let's get going. We should reach the school in a few minutes."

Ella glanced at Harebell Castle one more time before returning to the car. She still felt a little nervous, but now that she'd seen the castle she wanted to know what it was like inside!